Conghaile McLaughlin is a sociable, energetic, unique Irish, an up-and-coming author who resides in the heart of the historical Bogside, Derry City. Conghaile has a grasp of what is new and relevant when it comes to writing and creativity. His sparkling, one-of-a-kind personality purely does pour through the fine pages of his debut story: *The 'Joys' of Humanity.*

Conghaile McLaughlin

THE 'JOYS' OF HUMANITY

AUSTIN MACAULEY PUBLISHERS®

LONDON • CAMBRIDGE • NEW YORK • SHARJAH

A CIP catalogue record for this title is available from the British Library.

ISBN 9781035818396 (Paperback)
ISBN 9781035818402 (ePub e-book)

www.austinmacauley.com

First Published 2024
Austin Macauley Publishers Ltd®
1 Canada Square
Canary Wharf
London
E14 5AA

Chapter 1
Vivienne Westwood

Bright, blinding, electric Reno street lights radiated the city… all the colours were incredibly reminiscent of the "Nirvana" logo. The night was lustful, the moon was in full visibility. A rather tall looking woman, with angelic-white hair, excessive amounts of diverse jewellery, and a symmetrical face walked into one of Reno's vastly popular nightclubs in the 90s. This woman was Joy Monroe; she was a free force of pure nature! Residing just outside of Reno, Joy lived a lavish, wildcard lifestyle, she adored it! But most importantly… Joy loved the Metro.

The Metro was the name of the nightclub that Joy was walking into. It was purely popular in the 90s; every soul adored it! The club could hold up to at least 600 plus individuals! The decor was bluntly tacky, yet mesmerising to the eye. Lots of brown wood and spray-on gold!

Joy didn't have to wait in the huge queue for the nightclub. She avoided the mighty line of bodies because she usually spent three hundred dollars there, every Saturday!

She was valued… to say the least.

Joy's deal (in general) was that she worked hard, in her boring, draining accountancy job through the week… but evolved into an extremely insane party-animal at the weekends! This was Joy's routine; she adored it.

It was like she lived a double life: Dr Joy & Mr Party-Hyde!

Joy had a beautiful sense of style. She always looked the most sophisticated, slutty and stunning... all at once!

Her well-moisturised, several ringed fingers put on her luminous green wristband; this meant Joy was in the club, and intending on staying for a "while"!

The Metro was so big it had three levels: the drunken floor, for the drunks; the drugged floor, for the drug addicts... and the purge floor, basically for the nymphos who got lucky from the previous two floors.

Joy loved all three, but tended to stay usually on the first floor; with her trusty glass of double vodka, mixed with diet Coke.

That said alcoholic beverage gave Joy more hope and guidance than God ever had!

Diamonds may be basic female's best friends, but Joy Monroe's was a double vodka, whisked with diet-coke. Hell, the drink was her damn confidante!

There wasn't a certain "type" of person, when it came to the Metro. Hippies, ketamine addicts, pension receivers, women who were barely blossomed, hairy, obese men; everyone!

'Well... which one of your dolls is here tonight?' A lesbian, mullet-haired bartender asked Joy. The bartender wasn't Joy's friend, but she saw her every weekend without fail. More like acquaints. The bartender was named: Nancy, but she loathed that name, therefore making everyone call her by her nickname "Butcher"... because she adored a good bit of raw meat. Butcher asked Joy about which one of her "dolls" were out that night; she was referring to Joy's line-up of hook-ups that she always left the club with. 'Preferably one of the Latin ones...,' Joy replied back, as she took her drink and leaped over to the biggest dance floor.

The song playing was *Right Place Wrong Time* by Dr John.

Joy scoped, thoroughly; she was looking for someone to talk to... someone interesting. Gender was regardless. Joy needed someone to talk to.

In the dry corner of her hazel eye, Joy noticed a tall, long haired man sitting down on a velvet red booth, sipping on a Manhattan. Joy thought he pristinely looked like if Heath Ledger, and the fictional character, Paul Allen (from American Psycho) had a child together.

The admiration oozed off of Joy, by virtue of his glass of Manhattan! She knew he had impeccable taste once she rested her iris' upon him (and his cheap glass of orange alcoholic liquid).

She thought to herself *Fuck it*, deciding to prance over to him at the comfortable booth.

Her golden heels melted into the fabric of the booth's carpet.

'Hello,' Joy boringly exclaimed to the Manhattan-sipping man.

'What?' the man nastily replied.

'Excuse me?' Joy said back.

'Oh! My apologies, I commonly tend to act rough in front of a woman who is evidently superior to me... like yourself.'

Joy's eyes twinkled; he wasn't what she was expecting; 'You're a charm, Mr?' Joy asked/complimented.

'Joseph, the name's Joseph Kennedy.'

'I'm Joy.'

'I can already tell that. You're practically beaming with the emotion.' Joy knew in that instant that she had found her "Doll" for the night.

'I really admire your drink selection.'

'Thank you. In places like these, I like to stand out. Become unique; liquid-wise.'

'You're an intelligent man, Mr Kennedy.'

'Yeah, I get that off my uncles.'

'Who's your uncles?'

'John, Robert, Ted...'

'No fucking way!' Joy exclaimed in shock.

'Yup.'

'Your uncle's John F Kennedy?'

'Nah I'm kidding, they're my second cousins.' 'That's still rad. You're related to the Kennedy. What the hell!'

'They're cocks in real life.' Joy giggled at the spontaneous statement.

'In fairness, I did read an article that supposedly the dad of all the Kennedy's hated the fact one of his daughters lived a partying lifestyle, so he got her lobotomised.' 'Rosemary?'

'Maybe yeah.'

'Supposedly she had "violent seizures", but that's not the case. Patrick, their father was apparently a monstrous man!'

Joy was that enthralled with Joe's presence that she hadn't even realised she was standing up that whole time. 'Fancy a seat, Joy?' Joe asked.

'Wouldn't mind one, Joe.' The pair's chemistry was electric!

The Metro closed at 6.00 am. Joy glanced at the clock, whilst talking to Joe; the time 5.57 am! She was literally chatting to Joe for hours. The hours whisked passed her forehead; without her even realising!

'You know what I'm about to ask you, do you?' Joe oddly asked Joy; he was alluding to her coming back to his. 'It's almost time for me to be headed to my work, but thankfully I'm not in this week... so that's a yes to your cryptic invite.', Joe took a sip of his fifth Manhattan: 'Good, I'll get us a cab,' he exclaimed.

Joy quickly leaped to the female bathroom, as the club was closing in a literal minute. She crossed paths with "Butcher" on her journey.

'I guess you found your doll?' Butcher asked, Joy merely nodded; as she whizzed past the bartender, as Joy was painfully needing a pee...

As Joy left the toilet, then the club; she couldn't see her "Doll" anywhere. She got annoyed, as she waited for a few minutes.

Joy was painfully impatient.

A shockful poke was felt from behind Joy's waist. It was Joe.

'I've been scavenging for you everywhere!' he spurted.

'Well I'm here now. I was tirelessly waiting on you also!' Joy replied back.

At this stage, Reno was still fairly vibrant for being such a disciplined, alien time of day. There were the usual crack junkies and beggars looming around. But it was a Saturday night in Reno, in the early 90s. Think about it? There were sophisticated businessmen still out, models still out, housewives still out… the time might've been lonely; but the streets were surely not.

'Taxi!' Joe roared at an on-going cab driving by. 'Where do you think you are, a rom-com set in New York?' Joy asked.

'I apologise for trying to get a ride.'

'We'll walk,' Joy boldly offered.

'Walk? I don't know about you, but my shins would crumble into sawdust if I trekked 15 miles back to my home.'

'It'll be fun.'

'It most certainly would not!'

'Come on… have a bit of fun!' Joe gave in as he whirled through Joy's stunning eyes.

'Fine! But not my fault if you drop dead.' Joy laughed, gave him a quick kiss; then the pair both walked deep into Reno's Nightlife… even though morning was fast approaching.

'Joey! My boy!' an old, wealthy-looking, Al Pacino look alike yelled from across the street where Joe and Joy were…

'Marco O'Donnell?' Joe yelled back.

'Yeah, yeah it's me, ah good to see you,' Marco exclaimed as he crossed the road from the nightclub he was at. Marco was evidently Italian, but what puzzled Joy was that his surname was such an Irish name. She didn't have the courage to ask him why he had the surname (she should have the courage, as she was incredibly intoxicated).

Marco stepped onto the curb, away from the road. He reached vast into his pocket; finding a box of MS Italian cigarettes and a lighter.

'You don't mind if I light one near you, darlin'? You ain't a fuckin' snowflake, are ya?' Marco asked Joy in such a strong Brooklyn-Italian accent.

'No, you're fine; can I have a puff actually?' Marco inhaled his cigarette, blew the smoke away.

'Ah Joey boy finally got himself a good girl,' he also stated.

'What the hell are you doing in the Tube? I've never seen you in a nightclub,' Joe asked Marco.

'I decided fuck this shit, my old routine I mean darling and just went for a few with Bugsy and Pritchett. Last thing I know I'm out back of the club eating some young bitch's cunt as she stood on top of a steel rail, like raised up cannoli!' Marco replied.

'Wow…,' Joe stated.

'Quite a night then?' Joy asked.

'Haha, I like her Joey, I like her. You don't wanna stand on some steel rails, do ya hunni?' Marco asked Joy as he slowly approached her. Joe grabbed Joy.

'She's fine. Marc we needa' be get going. We'll see you,' Joe explained as Marc waved goodbye with a MS half-burned cigarette in his hand.

The pair walked further on. A rogue stone appeared, making Joe trip. His trousers went up his leg a little bit, showing some skin… as well as a tattoo of Vivienne Westwood's face on his shin!

'The fuck?' Joy asked, staring at his shin.

Joe quickly pulled his trouser back down.

'It's nothing,' Joe also said.

'It's clearly not nothing. That's definitely a tattoo of Vivienne fucking Westwood!' Joy frantically stated.

'It is a Vivienne Westwood tattoo. I was drunk, and decided to "spice up" my shin. A Vivienne Westwood tattoo was the best, I thought. God, you must think I'm a fucking freak.'

'I don't think that. But please let me see it.' Joe was hesitant to show her, but in the end he did. The tattoo was mildly small, but not hard to miss. The artist must've knew the elderly designer, because he tattooed her exact wrinkles & red hair dyed scalp! Joy couldn't help but explode with laughter. She apologised; as he rolled down his trouser once again.

'The really, really random tattoo adds to your uniqueness,' Joy complimented. Joe felt warmth within him. The 14-mile trek continued once more.

Let's not forget these two were drastically drunk, plus elated…

Hours flew by; it was now 09:00 am. They finally arrived at Joe's apartment; he lived beside a grand casino. The pair entered the building. Ding! The elevator bell gasped.

'After you,' said Joe.

'No, ladies first, Vivienne,' Joy said with a cheeky giggle. 'You're pushing it!'

Joe's apartment door was… weird, to say the least. He had a bulky, oaky, grey apartment door.

'Weird door,' Joy bluntly admitted.

'It was given to me by my dying, autistic aunt.'

Joy said nothing. 'I'm kidding. It scares away the Mormons, somehow,' Joe added.

Joy didn't really want to pander around his apartment, conducting irrelevant small-talk; she wanted to do one thing, and one thing only!

'This here's a…,' Joe said; talking about a wooden lamp, before Joy cut him off, to kiss him. They didn't waste any time. They marched over to his bedroom. They began their love making swiftly, because they'd been walking for almost four hours.

Joy thought the sex was magical; they went at it like heroin-addicted hyenas!

Eventually Joe passed out, due to all the drinks, drugs and sex.

Joy loomed out onto Joe's high-up balcony; noticing society among her was awake again. People in Reno were busy that Sunday morning.

Joy thought to herself it was time to go, she needed some vital rest. Most of the alcohol evacuated her system, by walking continuously, and sweating massively.

Before she left, Joy entered his kitchen to get a well-needed glass of h20. She was ready to leave, but she noticed a pen and three pieces of paper on a table. *Had to evacuate – was craving a sweet pretzel, Joy 17754189366* was read on a piece of paper, as well as the hand-drawn logo of Vivienne Westwood.

Joy's heels got whacked by fresh, brisk Reno air.

Her little cell phone began beeping. Her hangover wasn't bad. Yet Joy's classification as a "bad" hangover would be severe anxiety and a two litre bucket filled with vomit, to the normal alcohol consumer. Beep! beep! Joy's cell screamed. She couldn't find her phone anywhere in her deep, dark, leather bag. It continued to roar. 'Shut the fuck up!' Joy screamed at her phone, though it looked like she was screaming at herself.

'No, no you, sir,' Joy explained to an Asian man walking past, thinking she was roaring at him.

The cell phone was found. Joy thought that she would be receiving a call from Joe Kennedy; but rather Margaret Monroe; her mother!

Joy didn't hate her mother, she only hated her mother's personality ... Margaret Monroe was indeed the mom of Joy. Mrs Monroe wasn't really a classy woman, she rather enjoyed the simple, suburban things of life. Margaret would always say to her daughter: 'You should be out having me some grandbabies. Not settling down in the Dollar Store version of Las Vegas.'

The mother and daughter never saw eye-to-eye. It's no wonder they lived seven state lines away from each other!

Joy took a gulp; imagining it was a joint, then answered the call to her mother.

'Hello?' Joy faintly asked.

'It's me, your mother,' a torn-up Margaret replied. 'What's wrong, Mom?'

'It's your father, he's... he's been having an affair!' Joy's anger controlled her in that instant; but for both reasons: she was angry her mother rang her, when she was tired and hung over (slightly) to probably tell her another lie, because Margaret had poor mental health; also because the news of her father having an affair might actually be legitimate!

'M-mom, are you being serious?' Joy asked in an ascending panicking state...

'Of course I'm being serious, Joy. He's having a real affair, with a real middle-aged, fake-boobed housewife!' Margaret replied.

'Who is it?'

'Even her name makes me sick right up to my throat.'
'Answer the question, Mom!'

'Brenda Carson. He's having it with big-boobed Brenda…'

'Christian's mom?'

'Yes!'

'Where is Dad now?'

'Took a two-hour drive to a Walmart in Missouri, to get "fishsticks" that fucking man. If this is true, you know I'll need to come back home and confront him.'

'Stop it, Joy! You're sounding like I don't want my own daughter near me! And it is true, you never did believe a word I breathed after I white-lied to you, twelve years ago!'

'You told me my boyfriend committed suicide; then I almost died when I saw him walk into an Olive Garden in St Louis!'

'It was easier to tell a little, harmless lie; than to tell you he moved away in fear of getting some weird STD off of you.'

'I'm not going down this road again. All I'm saying is that if this is true, I'll be home really soon!'

'Good honey. Don't ring your father though.'

Joy had enough of talking to her annoying, insufferable mother, so decided not to ask why. 'I won't, Mom. I've gotta go; I'll call you when I book my flights.' Joy bidded. 'Okay, thanks honey. Don't forget to call me.'

"I won't, Mom. Bye.'". Joy then hung up the phone. Her head then began getting sore, after merely chatting to her own mother!

Her hand touched her painfully throbbing head. Joy began descending into more familial stress.

In the corner of her dry eyes, a taxi she did see; it was like a metal angel. Waving down the cab with great speed, Joy jumped into it with no thought whatsoever.

'Where to?' said the bald cab driver.

'Easton,' Joy replied.

Easton was just right outside of Reno. It was a small town; with a population of 300. Ironically, Easton was on the west of Reno. Joy lived in a small-ish home. But she didn't mind it.

Needing a rest, Joy slept as soon as she told the cab driver where to go… she didn't wake up until he told her they were outside her home! She jumped up like a Jack in a box.

'Sorry, how much do I owe you?' she asked, he pointed to the metre, with a big, visible scar on his hand. It read, *$320.14*. She felt wary about the price, but her head was still throbbing; so decided to give in and pay the sketchy cab price.

He beeped goodbye, leaving her staring at her door; reminding her of Joe's anti-Mormon door.

Her home was decorated classy; it was truly tasty.

Just wanting to take off all her jewellery; and go to sleep, Joy realised she had to book an economy ticket, to go back home…

Laid down like a lazy, long, lemur; Joy picked up her cell phone, rang Reno airlines – and shut her eyes as she booked a fairly cheap ticket to Table Rock Lake, Missouri.

Her ticket was booked for the day, Monday; at 09:00 am.

After hanging up the airline call, Joy finally rested; she slept like a succulent, oak log.

What a 24-hour time-frame Joy did have!

Chapter 2
The Female Mentality & Scotch

That infamous Monday morning did indeed arrive. Joy was ready, and packed for the airport. Her head was still a tad loopy/sore.

She hadn't received a phone call from Joe yet. That made her feel strange, as Joe didn't feel like any of her other "Dolls". She felt as if she got Joe, as a whole, perfectly.

But Joy didn't really look into the scenario, as all she was worrying about was getting to the flight on time, and her damned mother!

As a coping mechanism, Joy would do some digging into the latest, hottest, most popular gigs happening, whenever she felt bunged up with stress or anxiety etc… So as her cab pulled up outside her home in Easton, Joy got into the back; delving into several fliers she had, searching hard for the perfect gig to attend for when she got back to Reno. Call it looking to the future; avoiding the pressure…

Time flew by. Before Joy knew it, she was standing outside Reno's mediocre airport.

As she walked inside, the dirty, clammy airport air hit her up the face. She gazed over at the large information square, which gave out the times for flights. Joy's flight was in an hour. The snow-haired woman was thirstier than a rattlesnake on quale lodes; therefore, she bought a beautiful, freezing glass bottle of orange Fanta.

Joy had a second to herself; so she took a rest on a steel seat. She pondered to herself if Joe even put her number onto his phone, or if he forgot about her, or if she was in fact one of Joe's "Dolls". Eventually, the thoughts began annoying her, as she was overthinking.

The flight was then ready to board.

'Hello, good morning,' said a lovely flight attendant... She was too lovely for Joy's liking. The plane was roasting. All the seats were taken up. Joy's seat was at 14C. At her aisle sat a rather gorgeous looking raven-haired woman. She must've been in her early fifties; she was smoking a cigarette. Her style was greatly admired by Joy; and that's uncommon. The woman had just about the same amount of jewellery on her, as Joy did! She took a seat next to the stylish woman; oddly Joy felt intimidated; she didn't know why.

'Too warm in here,' Joy nervously said to the woman; trying to make conversation.

'I can handle my heat,' the woman replied back. Her cigarette's smoke polluted half of the plane's interior.

'Can I've a smoke?' Joy asked; trying to be cool, reminiscent of her asking Joe for a smoke of his cigarette. 'Yeah. Gone ahead.' The woman then handed Joy the cigarette. The cigarette was too tough for Joy's liking; therefore, she coughed heavily. In a raspy voice, she introduced herself to the woman,

'I'm Joy.'

'Hello honey, I'm Xanaithe Crawford.' the woman replied back.

'That's a stunning name.'

'You're too kind.' Xanaithe finished her cigarette. 'Where you headed too?' Joy asked Xanaithe.

'Going to see some sisters of mine.' said Xanaithe. 'I'm off to Missouri; my dad's apparently having an affair.'

Xanaithe giggled, and replied with, 'The show-me state, huh. I've been asked by a few married men if they could "show-me" their appendages, in that state.' Joy also laughed. 'I've got harder stuff in my bag if you're game?' said Xanaithe.

'For this flight, I'd take anything!' Joy replied. Xanaithe gently took out a small bag of pure Columbian cocaine, then smeared two thin lines with a golden credit card of hers. Then the glamorous woman sniffed her line in an instant, then nodded to Joy for her to take hers. Joy did, but just like Xanaithe's cigarette; her cocaine felt nothing like cocaine Joy had throughout the years! The presumably 56 year-old licked her golden American Express card clean; etching for every single last spec of the powder not sniffed. 'Can't be wasteful now, honey,' she justified. Both of them kept to themselves after taking the cocaine, until they landed, that's when Xanaithe admitted to Joy that she was cool. Joy appreciated what Xanaithe had said. Ms Monroe & Ms Crawford then bid farewell to each other. The flight was over – Joy wasn't ready to entangle with her mother… but the cocaine helped!

A rusty Chevy Caprice Classic (1995 model) pulled up outside the airport, in Missouri. The man inside the vehicle was awaiting Joy… it was her infamous father! The apparent cheat!

The man squinted out of his car's window; looking for his daughter. He wore distinctive club master glasses. Her father was named: Michael… His car was his pride and joy; his true mechanical love.

'There you are, Joy, Joy over here!' Michael yelled from within the driver's seat. Joy grabbed her luggage; as she walked to the Caprice Classic. 'Let me help, sweetie,' Michael insisted, as he got out to help with his daughter's luggage.

'Thanks, Dad,' Joy replied. The pair both got into the car, driving to Joy's former home, also her childhood home!

Table Rock Lake is an artificial lake, which isn't quite populated. Most who live within the Lake District mainly would off their daily businesses to the likes of Branson, or Shell Knob. The actual lake derives its name from a rock formation resembling a table at the small community of Table Rock… which is where Joy's parents reside, and where she grew up.

Michael glanced at his darling daughter. 'You're not your usual, chatty self?' he asked.

'Lot on my mind, Dad, Joy replied.

'You always told me everything that troubled you, that's until you moved to that Veno place.'

'Reno, Dad; it's called Reno.'

"Never mind what it's called. What's the matter?"–

Joy then took a deep breath in, and imploded onto her dad. 'Dad, the only reason I'm here is because Mom rang me yesterday saying that you're having an affair with big-boobed Brenda Carson. I know it's probably bullshit, but deep down this time I had inkling that Mom might be telling me the truth. This is the only week I get off from work, and I've been dragged back fucking here; so please tell me the truth, and nothing but the truth; because I quickly wanna get back to Reno to party my soul off!'

Michael was speechless; it was quite humorous in fact, because Margaret didn't even discuss the apparent cheating with her husband!

'I... I don't know what to say,' Michael replied back in shock.

'Just tell me if it's true, Dad?' An exhausted Joy asked.

'Of course it's not fucking true! What do you take me for? I have never once cheated on your mother! Let's recall it was her who did the dirt with a fucking Slovakian, six years ago!' Michael frantically expressed.

'I knew it... I'm sorry, Dad. I should've realised how nasty Mom can be.'

'It's fine honey. Margaret needs a reality check!' Michael squeezed his daughter's ringed hand, expressing love, also telling her not to feel guilty of assuming his apparent affair. The situation then nipped, as Joy & Michael drove back home; in a bid to confront their mother/wife... who was clearly not mentally well!

The sweet, baby blue lake tingled in Joy's eyes. She may have had a bad upbringing in Table Rock, but Joy adored the magnificent scenery.

'Your mother hasn't been well, you know. Ever since you left,' Michael admitted.

'What?' Joy replied; getting ready for a turbulent argument, following her father's snarky statement...

'Since you left for the sand, Margaret's been... "loopy".'

'What are you getting from this, Dad?'

'Nothing, sweetheart.'

'It sounds like you're guilt-tripping me?'

Michael took his specks off the road for a sec; looking at Joy. 'What? No! No, I don't mean that. Not for a second.' Joy looked back at her father in relief.

The long-awaited phone began to ring; it was indeed thee: Joe Kennedy! Joy panicked; she didn't know what to do. She thought of two options: option A, let the call slide and make Mr, Kennedy think that she was ignoring him, or option B, immediately answer the call and tell him that she wanted to hook up again real soon! Joy chose option A; letting the call die down, until the noise was no more...

'Who's the fella?' her father asked.

'Someone like you.'

'Someone like me?'

'Yeah. He's a guy who knows how to charm me, and make me laugh.'

Michael, himself, felt charmed by her statement. Because quite frankly, he was terrified his only daughter would turn on him, based on an apparent lie.

'Does he live in Reno too?'

'I don't actually live in Reno, Dad. I live in Easton, right outside of Reno.'

'I knew that.'

'You didn't know that.'

'I didn't know that.' Michael comedically replied.

Joy wasn't as open around her parents as she was in Reno. Like all young adults, truthfully. She was dying for a cigarette, but knew her father would cause a scene if he found out she smoked; because his younger brother: Sammy was a chain smoker, therefore leading to his throat-cancer diagnosis. For three short years, Sammy basically had no neck; it was visually disturbing. Sooner rather than later, Sammy died, leaving behind a heartbroken family, a box of hand-rolled cigs and a rusty lighter… Joy just decided not to purge her urge, meaning she didn't smoke at all near her parents on her trip back down memory lane!

The Caprice Classic pulled up right outside the house. It was beautiful. It was purely a classic, American home; with baby blue paint strips, as well as white woodwork, naturalistic ivy, plus much more…

A huge, deep breath came from Michael. Joy then copied, making her have a huge, deep breath.

'You don't have any cigarettes by any chance, do you?'

Joy howled with deafening laughter; as the irony took place. Michael loathed cigarettes, but scraping for any calmer for what's about to come, made the man need a cigarette! 'I do indeed have some.' Joy replied.

'I always reckoned you'd turn out a smoker.' Joy pulled out two from her crumpled up box, giggled; then lit them. The father-daughter duo huffed & puffed smoke for three minutes. Michael coughed quite heavily.

'Your first time, Dad?'

'Our Sammy ad his neck may have scarred me for life, but no not my fuckin' first time sweetheart.'

Joy then laughed heavily again. It was quite a bittersweet moment; great familial bonding…

The time then came; confronting her mother was long overdue, what follows next is purely toxic and bizarre!

Michael and Joy entered the house, Joy took a deep look around as she marched toward the kitchen, believing Margaret would be in there.

'Margaret, Joy's here,' Michael yelled. There was no answer from Margaret; she was nowhere to be seen. 'Honey… where are you?' Michael also yelled.

They looked all over the house, but she was nowhere… 'You call her,' Michael commanded Joy.

'No chance,' said Joy.

'Oh go on, you're her daughter; she'll answer to you…'

'Fine. Mom, Mom where are you? It's me, Joy.' There was still no answer! God knows where Margaret Monroe: AKA Mom could've been!

'This is getting boring now. Please just hurry up, and fucking appear!' Joy roared, losing grip of her patience.

Then, in the corner of her father's eye, Margaret was found at last! She was in the place the pair both forgot to look: the garden! 'There she is, Joy,' said Michael, pointing outside to his wife. Joy also looked out. The pair then went outside, via a glass door. Margaret was on all fours, planting some sort of purple flowers, with a half-empty bottle of scotch beside her.

'Mom?' Joy exclaimed.

'They're joys,' Margaret replied, not even turning her head to face them.

'They're joys? What are, Mom?'

'These little fellas. They are called alliums, but nicknamed "Joys", Margaret still didn't turn around to face her family, she only focused on planting the small, pretty flowers. Joy looked at her dad, in desperation.

'She's lost it, Dad… completely.'

'Margaret honey, please turn around to us, Michael pleaded.

'Get him away from me, sweetie,' Margaret roared to Joy, completely ignoring her husband.

'Why, Mom? It's not like he's done nothing wrong. I know you fucking lied about Dad cheating!'

Margaret then finally turned around. 'Don't you ever, ever, ever roar at me young lady!'

Margaret menacingly explained looking like a preying hyena, as her head was positioned like the "Kubrick Stare".

'You've lost it, Mom. It's actually madness!' said Joy.

'The only "madness" that's happening, is that your own dad is having an affair, is it that hard to understand!' Margaret screamed, whilst manically whacking her fingers onto her head, Joy got quite frightened; she'd never seen her mom like this before.

'I'm not having an affair, my darlin',' Michael desperately explained to Margaret.

'Don't let him speak to me, Joy.'

'Give me that first of all!' Joy said as she leaned down for the bottle of scotch…

'I think not, cursing at me is bad enough for you. Don't make me punish you like old times!' Margaret threatened as she squeezed her daughter's wrist painfully. Michael realised in that moment that his wife had completely lost her mind; it was so sad for him to witness. She made up a complete illusion, drunk heavily and brought up heavily traumatic memories to Joy, as Margaret used to violently whack Joy as a child. A rogue tear fell down Joy's powdered cheek, as she heard what her mother had said… the memories came flooding; they were not pleasant to say lightly! Feeling like a flamed bull, filled with anger, Joy clenched her fist.

'I wish you were fucking dead, you ginger old hag. I only came here to help you.' Margaret then also cried, whilst trying to hug her daughter. Joy swerved at her mom; as she got up.

'Honey I'm sorry!' Margaret explained, Joy merely ignored her.

'Where are you going?' Michael asked Joy, as she walked back into the house.

'As far away as her as I can; I suggest the same for you, Dad,' Joy replied.

Michael was swished with emotions; everything was happening so fast!

'I'm not well, Joy... please, I'm sorry,' Margaret exclaimed...

Swiftly Joy turned back. 'Yeah? Well guess what Mom, I'm not fucking well either. And who's fault do ya think that is?'

'I tried my best, sweetheart.'

'You were the worst fucking mother! I knew coming back to this hell-hole was a bad idea. Goodbye, Mom. I'll choose your coffin colour when the time comes,' Joy coldly said; finally leaving her damned childhood home, and her mother.

Outside, on the porch, Michael also left the house.

'I will, Joy. I will leave her,' Michael emotionally admitted. Joy deeply hugged her dad, as he began tearing up.

'She makes everything too real, Dad; she's not well,' Joy admitted.

Back in the home's garden, Margaret tried her utmost best to chug the rest of the scotch from the bottle; she got far enough, but ended up vomiting all over her beloved Joys. Sickeningly, Margaret vomiting on the purple flora symbolised her wrecking her relationship with her family.

The Caprice Classic started, Michael and Joy had nothing on their mind but their mother/wife. Michael wiped the last of his tears; beginning to drive.

Then, Joe Kennedy rang again!

Chapter 3
'Could This Be Dementia?'

Feeling flustered, Joy rolled down her father's car window. So many emotions/thoughts were rapidly flowing through her mind! The vulnerable young woman was overcome with complex emotion. Anger, confusion, rage, regret... were among the few!

'I'm sorry, honey...,' Michael honestly said; as he concentrated on the road.

'I'm sorry your mother rang you, I'm sorry she was so wicked... I'm sorry I didn't leave her sooner,' her dad also added.

Joy was then overwhelmed with nerves, and a sense of strangeness. Joy was (let's not forget) probably still violently hung over, rammed with trauma, filled with cocaine, amongst many other factors!

The woman decided not to pick up when Joe rang again; twenty minutes previous... she thought it was the right thing to do; but as time whisked by, her mind vastly changed!

Beep! Beep! Beep! Joy's phone miraculously screamed. Swiftly she checked to see who was ringing; it was indeed Joe! Without hesitation she answered!

'Finally you twit, who killed you? Or was I too boring for you to call?' Joe anxiously asked.

'No, nothing like that, you cretin. I had to go back home for a short while,' Joy replied.

'And "home" is where?'

'Table Rock Lake, Missouri.'

'God, sounds infested with Kenny Rogers super fans.' Joy couldn't help but laugh at that humour she barely knew but suddenly grew attached to.

'I got called by my mom.'

'Who? The schizo you despise and told you your ex-boyfriend killed himself, but was really alive?'

'Yes, exactly. How the hell do you know, Joe?'

'We walked half of Reno city, Joy. I could name every single one of your aunts and uncles. We were chatting nonsense for hours!'

'Rewind a minute. You described my wife perfectly!' Michael spontaneously spurted.

'I'm presuming you're this one's father?' Joe asked. 'I am indeed.' Michael yelled down the phone.

'Shit! Is your mom in the car? Did she hear me calling her a schizo?' Joe frantically asked.

'No, she's not in the car, and she won't be in our lives from now on, as she's nasty, plus selfish.' Joy explained. 'Bold… I love it.' Joy adored their conversation… It was like Joe Kennedy was vocally healing Joy from her turbulent encounter with her mother!

'Hey Joy, the Metro is hosting a gig for a heroin-addicted Aussie DJ named: Partiboi69. Wanna attend it with me?' Joe asked her.

She felt like a thirteen year-old again! Her heart was racing. 'Of course I'll go. It's in my local club, and there's a heroin-addicted Australian playing! What's not to love?' 'Perfect!' the long haired man replied down the cell phone.

'But what day do you come back from the black and white scene in the Wizard of Oz?' Joe also asked.

'That's a good question. Can my dad come too?' Joy humorously asked.

'Obviously!'

'Great, we'll see you in two days' time, Mr Kennedy.'

'Same to you two.'

'But when does it start?' Joy asked.

'Three days' time.' Joe explained.

'Fine. Bye…'

The pair then both hung up. Michael looked at his daughter heavily confused. Joy looked back at him. 'Hopefully there's no Margaret 2.0 at this heroin gig, honey!' Michael admitted.

Joy bursted out with laughter; her love for her dad intensified. He was not only road tripping seven states with her to get back to her home, but he was intending on living with her, and raving with her!

Joy's life may have crumbled with interaction from her mother, but enclosed within that Caprice Classic amongst her daddy, her life never felt better!

The pair pulled up outside a desolate gas station in Colorado. Michael was savagely craving a bottle of Schlitz (a supposed "beefy" flavoured beer)!

'This place better have Schlitz!' Michael muttered, like a child.

'Jesus, Dad. I've been hearing about Schlitz since Kansas!' Joy replied. Michael didn't reply to his daughter; merely rushed into the little store.

Inside the store dwelled the most horrific lightning the father and daughter had ever seen! It could've been mistaken for the large courtyard lights of Guantanamo Bay!

'Fuck!' Joy loudly expressed, looking at the lighting; whilst rubbing her large Vivienne Westwood necklace!

Michael scurried throughout the little store, he couldn't see the beer anywhere.

'Just one, I just need one!' Michael whispered to himself. Joy was a bit behind her father; she heard him whispering to himself.

'Dad! Quit talking to yourself. People will think you're a fucking crazy!' Joy commanded. Sadly, the beer was not in the store at all. Supposedly they hadn't sold that certain brand of beer since 1979! They found out this odd info by asking the main cashier: Sirenia, a fifty year-old with faint pink hair. Michael was distraught; God knows why he had such a hard hankering for the beer!

Nonetheless, the pair buckled up; heading back on the road, hopefully finding a cool, cold bottle of Schlitz somewhere along the way back to Reno city!

Quizzing herself, Joy asked her dad, 'Could this be dementia?'

'Could what be dementia?' Michael asked.

'The way Mom has rapidly changed her behaviour, and started descending into paranoia. I reckon she has dementia,' Joy thoroughly explained.

'Don't be ridiculous. Margaret may have some huge mental problems… but Jesus, I wouldn't go as far as bowing it down to dementia!' Michael expressed.

'In fairness, Mom has had a lot of dementia symptoms recently; even you can't deny that!'

'She may have some symptoms, not a lot; but the woman is fifty nine years-old!'

'Dementia can develop in younger years, not just elderly.'

'Quit it, Joy,' Michael then pleaded.

'Just think about it…'

The Caprice Classic then drove past a young mother dragging her son into preschool.

'I wonder where Mom is? Right now; at this very moment.' Joy also asked about her mother.

'Bingo, or in some other sort of hall… filled with women addicted to cookbooks.'

Joy giggled. 'You know, Dad. You've become instantly more funny, since you ditched Mom.'

Michael enjoyed the comment. 'Sweetie, if you keep mentioning the woman. All the comedy in me will disappear!' Joy laughed again…

Seconds, minutes and hours whisked by; as the pair drove straight past "The Silver State", Nevada board. Finally, Joy was home!

'It's… it's dry, Joy. But nice,' said Michael.

'Uh huh,' Joy barely replied, as she gazed at the surrounding weather, checking to see if there were fewer, or more clouds. She did this, because narcissistically, if there were less clouds in the sky; Joy could get laid easier! This was factual, because usually (pre Joe) Joy would leave the Metro with one of her "dolls", take them to an empty alleyway; make them look up at all the bold and beautiful stars and most definitely turn them on, as they looked up! She had it down to a fine art. But the real question was, could she use this explicit tactic with one: Mr Joe Kennedy?

Beep! Michael reversed up into Joy's home, in Easton. They then both got out of the car. It dawned on Joy that her father took nothing with him when they left Missouri!

'Dad. What about spare clothes, toiletries, etcetera?' she asked him.

'Oh I'll be fine. I've got money; quit the worrying,' Michael replied, easing his daughter from worry.

'It is a nice house!' he also sweetly added. They then went into the house; Michael inhaled a strong whiff of scotch! Joy went to her bathroom.

He felt disappointed in himself, as this was his first time ever entering his daughter's home (in such heinous conditions)!

'When does this gig start... Joy?' Michael yelled to his daughter; who was taking a piss six yards away.

'Um, I dunno actually. Joe didn't specify,' Joy replied.

'We'll need to not be late!'

'Why are you in such a hurry?'

'Because the women my age, that's if there will be any; will usually go earlier, and leave earlier.'

'Dad, it's the Metro. I once saw a woman in a zimmer frame sniff a line of ketamine and suck the face off someone.'

'I hope you mean kissing!'

The time was then: seven thirty. They were both clean + showered.

'I'm sorry, Dad, but this is the only male clothing I have in here,' said Joy, as she held up a pair of purple cargo pants and a black hoodie, with Elvis Presley's face on it!

'That really all you got?' Michael desperately asked. 'Yeah. Some bald guy left his clothes here after we had sex. He must've ran home naked!'

'Fine,' Michael said, as he grabbed the odd clothes – which weren't suitable for the event, 'But I really do question who you fuck!' he also added.

Joy felt… free. Not happy, sad, or negative. But simply… free.

Her mind blew up, thinking she'd look attractive in her trouser suit!

The pair were then ready. Ready to party!

'I'll ring a cab,' Joy said, Michael agreed, whilst glancing at her hand which was holding her phone.

'Dear lord, Joy! That amount of jewellery?' he asked. 'Jewellery attracts money… and friction.'

Honk! An oddly sounding horn roared.

Michael was ecstatic to see all the life and fun Reno had to offer. People were everywhere! It was a vast change from the same three local bars he would socialise in, back in Table Rock Lake.

The fare came to sixteen dollars; Michael paid.

The queue to the Metro must have been at least stretching two blocks!

'We'll be here, waiting till next Spring!' Michael worried.

'Oh no we won't,' Joy said, as she easily walked past the several bouncers with her dad!

'How'd we get in so easily?' her dad asked.

'I spend more than those bouncers make a month in here, every Saturday. Somewhat of a VIP, I don't know whether to hug or give off to you.'

They got a few drinks and stayed on the first floor. "The Drunk Floor", hoping to see Joe, as she didn't ring him, to let him know she was on her way; and vice-versa!

Michael looked down at his hoodie and odd pants; he worried that the attire he was wearing was inappropriate. But, he then realised individuals were wearing far worse, plus far less than him!

Creeping up on Joy, like a retched, dry beetle, the "Butcher" welcomed Joy back into the nightclub.

'Who's he?' the mullet-haired woman bluntly asked. 'My dad,' Joy replied.

'Seriously?'

'Yeah.' the "Butcher" then looked at Michael as she shaked his hand.

'Hello, I'm Joy's dad, Michael.'

'Hi, Michael, if you need a drink or five, just let me know, okay?' said the "Butcher".

'I like this place already,' Michael replied.

Joy then thought she caught a slight glimpse of Joe's long hair, so she grabbed her dad and said "bye" to the "Butcher".

She hunted the dance floors like a feral fox, who got a slight sniff of meat!

'I can't find him, Dad.'

'It's not that big of a place.'

Joy merely looked at her dad.

'Fine. I take that back. It's an okay size to track someone down,' he added.

Michael gazed away in the opposite direction, for a hot second; he noticed a woman (who he presumed was around his age; her wrinkles admitted her year of birth), who looked rather attractive.

'Joy, darling, I'm headed over this direction. Hopefully you find your man,' Michael states, as he just up and left his daughter, heading towards this more "vintage" female! Joy was shocked, but continued to search for Joe, like a crazed huntress!

There were six bars situated on each floor of the Metro. That means within the club, there were eighteen bars altogether! If that doesn't create a scope of how big the club was, then nothing will.

She could not find him anywhere! So she decided to strut over to one of the bars on the floor she was on (the drunk floor). The bartender didn't ask what she was having, he merely nodded his head up, as a way of lazily asking what she was after.

'Double vodka with Diet Coke,' said Joy. The drink was made; Joy took a deep gulp and turned ninety degrees to see if she could finally see the man she had been dying to see!

Sadly, she could not…

One hundred yards north of Joy, her dad was right behind a woman who caught his eye, he decided to fake a cough, getting her attention. The woman turned around to face Michael.

'Sorry, am I in your way?' she asked.

'No. But I was just admiring your necklace,' Michael replied.

The woman wore the exact same necklace that Joy wore, the pearly Vivienne Westwood!

'Why thank you. I'm Veronica,' Veronica said, as she held her hand out shaking Michael's.

'Michael.'

'Hello, Michael. I may say though, I do not admire that hoodie of yours.' Michael laughed at what Veronica had said.

'My daughter packed it for me, she's over there somewhere.'

'A daddy-daughter party duo... I love it!'

The pair hit it off like two old flames rekindling.

Joy's double vodka and Diet Coke was empty; she sunk it swiftly.

His face was finally seen by Joy!

'Joe! Joe! Over here, it's Joy! She screamed like a child wanting a Barbie doll. Joe couldn't hear Joy with all the noise around him. He had two drinks in his hand, Joy anxiously worried that the second beverage was for another woman! But as she followed Joe, she realised he was giving the second drink go his colleague, the no-filter, Brooklyn, Italian, Irish-surnamed: Marco O'Donnell. Joy realised who the man was, because when Joy and Joe were walking back to his apartment, they bumped into him.

Taking a big gulp, Joy walked over to their booth! The club's lights were blinding the woman, but she finally made it over to Joe's booth.

Joe instantly noticed Joy walking toward his booth.

'Joy!' Joe addressed.

'Hey,' Joy awkwardly replied.

'Eh, did we meet before?' Marco asked Joy. 'Um...'

'Yeah, you both met each other recently,' Joe interrupted.

'How have you been, Joy. Since you know...,' Joe asked.

'Shockful, but the double vodka will help', Joy replied. Joe laughed at her statement; as he hugged her, grabbing her hip. Marco O'Donnell saw Joe gripping Joy's hip; he then thought he'd make an exit from the booth, "Joey boy I'll chat to you later, and nice seeing you, Joyce", Marco explained as he left to venture deep into one of the vibrant, colourful dance floors. "He's old. He forgets everyone's names", Joe exclaimed, in Marco's defence.

Joy's pearly blue eyes looked directly into Joe's brown pools of youth.

'Why did you invite me here tonight?' Joy asked. 'Because I wanted you here.'

'You knew I'd inevitably be here... so why ring me and invite me?'

'Because let's not forget a certain someone left their cell-phone number and a little, cute hand-drawn logo of Vivienne Westwood on my table!'

'You know what point I'm trying to make.'–

'Oh I know, but I much rather like the point I'm about to make,' Joe said as he grabbed Joy's neck; emotionally kissing her!

Their passionate saliva-swap lasted a whopping three minutes!

'I'm thirsty as fuck. We should head for a drink,' Joe said to Joy.

'Yeah, I agree,' Joy replied.

The song *Material Girl* by Madonna began playing in the club; everyone at that time adored the bouncy tune! The majority were energetically dancing...

Joy and Joe then leaned up against one of the bars; Michael was also leaning up against the same bar, kissing the face off of the woman he was chatting to, Veronica! Joy witnessed this and her throat gulped with shock! Quickly she nudged Joe.

'Look over there! That's my fucking dad sucking the face off of some woman!' Joy explained.

'That's Michael?' Joe asked with a subtle giggle, 'Yep! That's him!'

Michael then took a break from kissing Veronica; he put his middle and index finger up, miming that he wanted two venom's to the bartender.

His head turned over to the left; he noticed his daughter and thee Joe! Humorously Michael smiled and pointed at his weird hoodie; kind of visually telling the pair that even with a horrid outfit, he could still get off!

Michael told Veronica to then look over, she did and she waved as she wiped her thinish lips.

His wrinkled hands grabbed Veronica's mature waist; leading her over to his daughter… thus creating a completely intoxicated sociable foursome!

'So you're the infamous other half of the daddy-daughter party duo?' Veronica asked.

'Indeed, I'm Joy.'

'And you must be Joe!' Michael asked Joe.

'Of course.'

Michael then tightly hugged Joe, as well as giving her a big sloppy kiss on her cheek. Michael pointed at the large Elvis Presley face that was ironed onto the odd hoodie that he was wearing within the club.

'What's the deal with your outfit?' Joe asked Michael, in the nicest way he could.

'Blame her!' Michael replied; pointing to her daughter.

Veronica spontaneously strummed her fingers through Michael's sweating, drunk scalp.

'Calm down, Margaret!' Michael accidently spoke to Veronica.

'Margaret? Who the hell's Margaret?' Veronica angrily/rapidly replied.

'No one. I meant your name,' Michael redeemed. 'Are you fucking cheating on Margaret!' Veronica roared.

'Margaret doesn't exist! I meant Veronica!' Michael deliberately lied... the four stood still, plus silent for a thirty seconds; 'Who wants a shot of Sambuca?' Michael asked; trying to break the frosty tension, Joy fixed her hair and she agreed to some Sicilian shots.

Veronica must've been on some drugs... or genuinely was a mad woman, because after Joy agreed to shots, Veronica literally jumped in the air, hugged Michael, and explained to him.

'Margaret's a lovely name!' The remainder, which included Joy, Michael and Joe, was astonished at how crazy this stranger was. Just because they knew her name and Michael shared a kiss with her, didn't mean they even knew anything about her!

Michael decided to not tell the looped Veronica that he was still married to his even more looped wife: Margaret!

'Four Sambucas! The Sicilian kind,' Joe asked a bartender, as the group of four stood around the bar awaiting their beverages.

The Metro's shot glasses were larger than ordinary shot glasses. They were a few inches taller!

'Three, two, one!' They all yelled as they downed their bitter shots. Joy innocently wiped her lips; she loved shots of Sambuca! For four, the cost was twelve dollars.

Suddenly, Joy had the urge to use the restroom; Veronica went with her (to the bathroom). The woman her father was kissing was clean mad!

The club only had one smoking area.

Joy then had a sudden urge to smoke a cigarette, after she used the bathroom.

Veronica didn't follow her to the smoking area; the woman went back to the dance floor to Michael and Joe.

Joy's ringed left-hand pushed open the wooden door which divided the sweaty dance floor and the ashy smoking area.

The place was cold, but the ungodly amounts of cigarette smoke mildly heated the area up!

Her mind boggled. '*Who can I scram a cigarette off?*' she thought to herself.

A rusty, dusty old speaker accommodated the smoking area. It sat upon one of the metal rails which made the ceiling. Music sang out of it… but it was mumbled and grainy.

Joy's heels were ever so shortly getting dirty, because she kept standing on smoked, burnt cigarettes. At that point tough, Joy didn't care; her main priority was smoking a glorious, regret-free cigarette.

She spotted a transgender woman holding a box of Camel cigarettes. Joy didn't usually smoke Camel's… she was more of a Marlboro girl!

'Excuse me, would you have a spare cigarette by any chance?' Joy asked the woman.

'Oh yeah, of course,' the woman replied.

Joy didn't even interact with the woman after she got a cigarette off her. She usually would; as a sociable way of saying thanks for the spare cigarette; but Joy was gasping a smoke that much that she just yanked the cigarette off the transgender woman, and smoked it there and then!

Joy smoked it till the very bitter end of the but!

Relaxed Joy did feel.

'Thank you so much!' Joy exclaimed to the woman. She must've felt as if she gifted Joy a million dollar bills, with how emotional Joy did sound as she thanked her.

Then back upstairs she went, scouting out for her complex flame: Joe Kennedy, her middle-aged father: Michael Monroe and a random, eccentric woman: Veronica (surname not known)!

The dance floor was inevitably packed...

Twenty brief minutes flew by. The time was now: 03:15 am!

Joy could not find her group anywhere! It was like a repeat of the start of the night, when she could not find Joe Kennedy.

Her mind had to act fast; as she realised they were definitely not downstairs. Joy decided to check the Metro's second floor: the drugged floor!

The drugged floor was obviously for people who wanted to take drugs. Her dad never did drugs, so it must've been Joe or mad Veronica's idea to take a trip upstairs, for some cocaine, meth or god knows what!

For display purposes only, the Metro had a spiral staircase that did indeed lead to the second floor of the club, but not one being (who's deeply intoxicated) would venture up the spiral staircase. The club did obviously have a logical set of stairs that led directly to the drugged floor.

Joy stumbled up the stairs.

Joy was unfamiliar with most drugs, she usually only did marijuana and sometimes cocaine. The stench of the pure marijuana ambushed Joy; it's all she could smell as she entered the drugged floor.

The floor was also rammed with people. Mostly they all looked like a blend of stoners, energetic businessmen and stressed mothers of fours!

'*The owner of this club must be a fucking billionaire!*' Joy thought to herself, as she truly realised how busy her local nightclub does be; every single weekend!

Michael's Elvis Presley hoodie was printed out weirdly; Joy realised this as the club's lights were reflecting onto the Elvis face. She found them! With the help of what her father was oddly wearing.

'Dad!' Joy yelled loudly towards her father. Michael did surprisingly hear her daughter yelling. He pointed at the group, as Joe was buying a white substance off a man with a ponytail.

Joy sighed; walking over to them.

Joe's eyes were completely bloodshot. Iron walls of scarlet completely polluted Joe's white eyes. The substance was definitely not cocaine…

'The drugged floor, really Joe?' Joy asked Joe. 'Come on, Joy. We were bored downstairs,' Joe replied. 'What the hell's that drug?' Joy also asked Joe.

'It's only a little bit of heroin.'

'I didn't have any, don't worry, Joy,' Michael assured his daughter.

'Well I did. And that's some great fucking stuff!' Veronica said, as she coughed violently.

'Would you like any… Joy?' Joe asked gently; thinking she'd say no.

'Okay. Fuck it!' Joe madly replied!

Joe, Michael and Veronica looked at each other. They evidently knew that Joy did some light drugs, class A. But they didn't recon she'd agree to take the heroin among them! Joe then whipped out the small spoon he formerly put in his pocket. It was obvious that the spoon had been through some substance-intake endeavours! Mr Kennedy then took out the bag containing the powder. His eyes wrapped around Joy's.

'You sure you want this?' he asked her.

Joy nodded confidently. The dim flame deriving from his green lighter gently lit up the white powder. It was melted down, within the pan. Joe then finally took out the menacing syringe. Joy knew he wasn't an amateur, because the syringe was his own and it didn't have a little Reno hospital logo on it. Joe's hand daggered the blade into Joy's aquatic vein. She felt a whirlwind if emotion; she hadn't touched that stuff in a brave while!

Everyone comforted Joy, as if she did something admirable/respectable; instead of literally doing some raw heroin!

Her mind felt heavy.

Complexly the heroin made her full of life… but dull simultaneously…

Michael was indeed telling the truth when he admitted to not taking any of the heroin. He was severely drunk though. He didn't feel guilt for watching his daughter take some seriously dangerous drugs.

'How'd you find that?' Joe asked Joy about the drugs.

'Weird,' Joy responded as she giggled heavily. Joe knew the heroin began to work as she acted "weird".

'More drinks I think!' Veronica asked; applying more thick lipstick.

'Of course!' Joy replied with her eyes as wide as the Golden Gate Bridge!

A huge thud came from the entrance of the drugged floor. It was Marco; he must've got bored of the first floor also. His hair was a mess. He still looked identical to Al Pacino, but a messed-up hair version... the thud came from Marco banging into the wooden. Marco didn't look like Joe Pesci (another actor famous for the mafia film genre) but he did act like him; hot-headed and short tempered! He began booting and roaring at the door; he must've thought the door was a real person who bumped into him (where in reality, he was the one who bumped into the door)!

'For fuck sake, I can't get a break from this guy!' Joe expressed as he witnessed Marco arguing with an inanimate object!

'Who's the guy?' Veronica asked as she also saw Marco arguing with the door.

'He's a colleague of mine.' Joe Kennedy had to admit.

'He needs a reality check,' Veronica hypocritically said, as she herself needed a reality check!

'You know, he looks like that actor in Heat,' Michael admitted.

'Al Pacino!' Joe and Joy both said to Michael at the same time.

Joe decided to just try and ignore him, as his vision couldn't be that superior if he's banging into and arguing with wooden doors.

Ironically, the four individuals came to the Metro that Saturday for DJ Partiboi, but ended up not paying attention to him at all!

Two hours whisked by, the time was now 05:44 am!

Marco still hadn't seen them…

The Metro at that time was beginning to empty, people had enough of booze, dancing and drugs for one night; Joy felt the same, so she told everyone she was leaving.

Deep within her devious mind, Joy didn't really want to go home, but much rather go to Joe's home! Her plan succeeded.

'I'll come with you!' Joe said as she then hugged him. Michael sort of had to tag along, as Veronica was blacked out on a dirty booth.

As the three were leaving the drugged floor, Marco squinted over at them.

'Who's that?' he asked out loud; Joe put his hand on his lip, meaning for them to be quiet and keep walking downstairs so Marco doesn't know who they are.

Even the first floor was empty…

Eventually, the left the Metro nightclub and got whacked up their faces with fresh, morning air!

'Please tell me you have a cab!' Joy asked Joe, as she didn't want to repeat last Saturday! His response was kissing her.

'Of course I do!' he simply assured Joy.

The cab came and went. Before they knew it, the three of them were standing in front of Joe's weird apartment door.

Michael didn't even utter a word when he went inside Joe's apartment. He decided to just sleep in one of Joe's spare rooms.

Joy took a defined look around Joe's apartment.

Eventually, Joy's eyes lined up with Joe's... as he stared at her.

'I got a new mattress,' Joe plainly admitted. 'Waterbed?' Joy asked.

'Go in and find out,' Joe cheekily expressed.

Joy did; she walked into Joe's bedroom. It was true! Joe bought a 70s waterbed!

Her fake facade expressed that she thought the waterbed was tacky and cheap, but internally Joy adored the waterbed. It was edgy, diverse and different!

Joe playfully hopped upon the bed made of H20 – Joy didn't jump onto the bed, for if she did then she'd bust it open; with all her jewellery.

Intense love-making was undoubtedly made!

They went for seven erotic, romantic, fantastic rounds of intercourse!

In Reno, the city's equivalent of a cockerel waking people up was a crack head yelling at a liquor store owner because he didn't have any chocolate Twinkies in-stock!

The yelling woke both Michael and Joe...

Michael's mind was heavy and sore. He exited the spare room scratching his hair.

Joe also left his bedroom feeling dead.

The pair encountered each other in Joe's kitchen.

Joe's golden watch blinded Michael, as Joe poured himself a glass of orange juice, as the morning sunshine reflected into Michael's eye; via Joe's glamorous golden watch.

'Sorry 'bout that,' Joe Kennedy said as he finished pouring his OJ.

'No, you're fine. My head feels worse than it ever did listening to my crazy ex-wife all those years!' Michael honestly admitted to Joe...

'Veronica?' Michael also asked, Joe looked right at Michael and rabidly howled with laughter...

'She was insane, man!' said Michael.

They both screamed and cried with pure laughter, as they reminisced about the insane night out they had the night before.

'Can you two keep it down for god's sake!' Joy pleaded as she still slumbered in Joe's bedroom.

They even laughed at Joy being annoyed at them.

Laughing, whilst trying to whisper is extremely difficult; Michael and Joe would know... as they had to as their daughter/fling was trying to get some hangover rest!

Eventually Joy woke up, she didn't feel anxious, she didn't feel depressed, she didn't feel excited: she only felt like she wasn't there!

The feeling she felt was absolutely terrifying to her! She had never felt like this before!

Her emotions, her surroundings, her reality all felt... disconnected!

She didn't know how to handle it.

It was an alien emotion; she felt like she wasn't there.

It was as if she was living in a dream or a film.

As she continued to hear her dad and Joe laugh, she felt nothing. Nothing amused her, nothing sensate her. She was scared, scared for herself.

This new mental state literally creeped up on Joy Monroe, as she woke up that fateful Sunday!

Tears dripped down her face.

She left Joe's apartment.

She left without her clothes, without her father and without her grip of reality!

Chapter 4
Depersonalisation / Derealisation Disorder

Life felt like a haze for Joy…

She didn't know what she felt like, but she sure didn't feel normal!

The brisk morning air woke Joy up. She genuinely thought she was in a dream. She waited so desperately to be awoken. Her bare, cold feet just kept walking. She didn't get awoken; because she wasn't in a dream!

When she left Joe's apartment, she ran out of the place; like a disassociated cheetah.

She ran so far that it was highly unlikely that her dad or Joe would find her, or catch her.

The strangest thing for Joy was that she was perfectly aware that she wasn't losing her mind. She knew she was there, but felt like she wasn't. She felt disconnected from the environment!

Her wrist wiped her on-going tears.

The white-haired woman was indeed bombarded.

She wouldn't wish this feeling on anyone.

Visually, her eyesight was perfect all her life, but suddenly everything was a tinge blurry!

Her fragile mind couldn't take it!

The pedestrians funnily enough didn't notice Joy was barefoot, with only her shirt and skirt on. They all were used to seeing these kinds of people. Everyone put her down as being just another crack head!

Joy couldn't even look people in the eye. Everything felt off, fake, distant!

It was the heroin Joy thought to herself. *It was the heroin, it's raw. No wonder I feel this odd*, she also thought. She had it down to a tee, thinking the heroin caused this scary mental state. Deep down within her fractured, disconnected mind was hope, hope that she would be fine after she takes a sleep… but sadly she wasn't fine, as two months went by and Joy was still in this dream-like state!

Joy blocked Joe out of her life straight after she left his apartment. She loathed the man, as she thought he was the culprit of making her like this! She told her dad all about how she was feeling; he felt nothing but guilt. He thought he and his ex-wife: Margaret were the reason. But honestly no one knew what was the source of this odd feeling.

Joy would soon find out though, as she booked an appointment with a counsellor 2 months' prior; the time for the counselling had then come!

Shockingly also, Joy hadn't attended the Metro Nightclub in two months!

She tried everything! She cut out alcohol, drugs, bad foods, everything! In a hope to rid this disconnected feeling… nothing worked though.

It was a Tuesday. Michael was still living with his daughter, in her home. They pair hadn't heard a peep from Margaret ever since they left Table Rock.

Her father was so overwhelmingly stuffed with guilt! He felt as if he and his ex-wife were the sole reason for Joy's newfound state.

Joy sat on her grey couch. She looked down at her feet and hands; she felt as if they were not part of her! She twisted her hands, then moved her feet in a circular motion.

Michael was in the kitchen. He was brewing a cup of coffee.

Joy didn't even intake caffeine for two months... as she thought the drug/stimulant could be helping to cause the isolated mental state.

Her kitchen was vastly populated by veggies.

Joy tried and cut out everything; hoping to merely get back in touch with her normal state + reality!

Her television was playing a season 8 episode of the Golden Girls.

Her emotions were numbed; she hadn't felt genuine excitement, love or joy in two whole months!

She decided to blend up a smoothie consisting of kiwi and cherries.

Her blending machine was tacky. It was made of cheap plastic and spray painted gold. In fairness though, the "NINJACUT" did carry out its job brilliantly; taking the edge off Joy's constant hangovers.

Mrrrrrrrrrr! That was the noise the blender made. 'Is it nice?' Michael awkwardly asked, Joy couldn't hear him – so he thought she was ignoring him... as you look back, Michael Monroe was indeed a severely anxious man!

With the way Joy was feeling, it was a strenuous task to merely look people in the eye!

Acting like a distant robot, Joy plainly took out another glass, poured the leftover smoothie into the spare glass and gave it to her father; not uttering a peep.

Joy obviously realised she couldn't block her father out, like she did with her mother.

'This appointment is soon. I'm gonna go get ready... see you later,' she emotionlessly said to Michael. Even the way she formulated her sentences were none other than: soulless!

Michael had to do something. It was terrifying him to see his little girl feel and act like that! He tightly hugged his darling Joy. He hoped with every inch of pure optimism within him that the hug would somewhat ground his daughter back to reality! Joy predictably did/felt nothing...

She then left the kitchen, where she then headed to get ready for her first ever counselling session!

Michael was never really a religious person, but ever since Joy acted distant and dissociated Michael prayed... he prayed hard and long!

Joy decided to wear a light green trouser suit. The counsellor was situated in the upper east side of Reno. In a big, ivy-covered building named: Clarendon Manor.

Joy drove there.

Her predictions of what Clarendon Manor would look like, included Arkham Asylum, some haunted building... or a gateway to hell!

She was wrong though, as were her predictions. The manor was lovely. It was filled with flora. Ivy was everywhere. It genuinely was a bright, beautiful, authentic building. But the real question was, was it going to be swell and sweet inside?

Wind appeared. Joy's hair went everywhere.

Her mind decided to take one valiant step out of her car; she physically fell through with it, as she left her motor and entered Clarendon Manor!

The reception was bright. The main office was like an island on the marble floor; it was a circle office.

'What's your appointment?' the male receptionist asked Joy, with a sturdy Bronx accent and chewing gum. 'In fifteen minutes,' Joy replied back with a slight rude tone, as she thought it was justified as the Bronx receptionist was quite blunt to her – the receptionist didn't speak then; he just pointed to a seat for Joy to sit in…

The vibrant reception had a single framed photo of the former president: Richard. E Nixon, on a blue painted wall which had a door leading to a long hallway of rooms.

How does an old, ignorant Republican get a picture framed in this place? Joy thought to herself as she played with one of her steel rings which rested upon her right index finger.

'I guess he was the president, but a mediocre one at that,' Joy in depth argued with herself.

As she gazed around the room, she noticed everything getting blurry; as if there was an emotional filter on her sight.

Deep down she knew she was in reality, and she was real… but she felt a million light years away!

All Joy wanted was to feel connected with everything again…

Time didn't whiz by, if anything it dragged like a crazed lunatic dragging a bloody sledgehammer across a concrete ground.

Joy thought about her mother, about how Joe was feeling and how she was going to get out of this dissociative state!

Joy watched hazily as the male receptionist got off his seat; walked over to Joy and said her name two times as she felt extremely unfocused + dissociated.

'Ma'm! Ma'm! Dr Irwin's ready for you now,' the receptionist yelled to Joy – Joy then shook herself and replied with a mere nod, as her disassociation made her not want to communicate with individuals (or even look them in the eye)!

Joy then picked up her stylish, leather hand bag and walked in the direction of the corridor, where the framed picture of Nixon rested.

'Third right,' the receptionist bluntly stated to Joy.

Her ringed hand opened the white painted door.

'Oh! You're exactly on time! I admire that!' the therapist, Dr Irwin said to Joy. She was a red-headed, lovely smelling, glasses wearing woman, who evidently adored the colour purple; as her whole office was purple! The walls were purple, the desk was purple, the chairs were purple, even the United States of America flag was purple! Yes, really.

Dr Irwin had a seventies conversation pit installed into her office. Could you guess the colour of the chunk of ground that was lowered to form more space and seats? It was purple. The pit was awkwardly placed into the office, as there wasn't enough room for a beneficial conversation pit. It looked more like a hole to grow purple potatoes than a boogie concept from the seventies!

'Can I ask for your name?' the doctor asked.

'Joy Monroe,' Joy replied.

'Stunning name.'

The therapist had too much energy; it couldn't have been natural. Within Joy's clouded mind she thought of a joke with genuinely made her laugh.

This girl must be on the same stuff which made me fucked up! Joy thought to herself humorously.

Dr Irwin's first name was ironically Jean. It was ironic that her first name was Jean because the doctor looked strikingly similar to that of a Marvel comic book character: the powerful mutant Jean Grey...

'On the phone you mentioned the big bad D word.' Dr Irwin asked Joy.

'Big bad D word?'

'Yes! Depersonalisation/Derealisation Disorder!'

'Oh yeah. I did mention that on the phone.'

'I hate that word, honey. I prefer to use the term "walking", "How come?"'

'Well, I believe that big word Depersonalisation/Derealisation Disorder frankly immediately labels people as robots almost.'

Joy was confused and Dr Irwin noticed that. 'Look, I know you're confused, but using the term "walking", as in your brain walking away from reality, instead of using the actually daring title is just more beneficial. Do you get me?'

'I do, actually!' Joy replied to the therapist.

Dr Jean Irwin grinned with a set of milky white, completely straight gnashers.

'How do you feel, Joy? And I mean really, how do you feel?' Irwin asked Joy.

'I feel as if I'm not here. I'm aware I'm really here, but I feel as if I'm not. I feel blurry, I feel fake, I feel as if living in a video game is the norm for now... I feel disconnected,' Joy spurted.

'Okay, classic symptoms of "walking", Irwin replied.

'When did the symptoms begin?' Irwin elaborated. 'Around two months ago.'

'Fine. Do you believe you could roughly pinpoint a trauma or change within your life which could've spiked the 'walking' or anxiety, stress etcetera?'–

'I think it's a culmination of having a really bad drug trip, large alcohol intake and remembering childhood trauma I worked so hard putting behind me.'

'That's okay. Would you mind elaborating firstly on the drug trip, please?'–

'Fine. I took really dodgy heroin two months ago... and it completely changed me. It was terrifying. Sometimes I wonder if it was actually even heroin or rather some voodoo dust from Hati!'–

Dr Irwin giggled and stated to Joy, 'Your humour is a vital reason as to why we're going to get you cured and back in touch with reality!'–

'Do you drink every day, Joy?' Irwin also asked. 'No, but I have a job with my local bar: the Metro so I get free booze and usually drink large amounts at the weekends.'–

'Okay,' Dr Irwin plainly replied, as she wrote into her little black book. 'Finally, you mentioned you suddenly remembered childhood trauma. What did you mean by that?'–

'My mom and I, uh never got along. She's got severe mental health issues. She mentally neglected me as a child. To cut a long story short, my mother rang me two months ago lying to me about my father having an affair, purely to cause chaos and gain attention. I stupidly believed her, so travelled back to my childhood home, when I found out as suspected that my father was not having an affair. I confronted my mother, then she uttered words that a younger me would've wetted herself at. She said to me dead in the eye, "Don't make me punish you like old times". I know it doesn't sound very menacing or threatening but her tone, her face, everything purely shook me to the core. After she spoke those words to me I immediately disowned the woman I formerly called Mom. Also my father left my mother that day and ever since he has been living with me, so that too adds to my "walking".'

'You've had the run of the mills this past while, eh?' Joy nodded. 'I agree with you, Joy, all the newfound change, stress and past trauma, as well as the heroin has indeed created a new coping mechanism within your mind. I would most definitely consider that you have DPDR, better known by me as "walking".'

That was it. Joy was diagnosed (not officially, but strongly). She felt shocked.

'I know now there is definitely a history of negative mental health in your family, with being your mother, but are there any other traces of mental health, your father's side for instance?' Dr Irwin inquired.

'My uncle, my dad's brother drank himself to death and my mother's mother, grandma Beverly was bipolar. One night my grandma had a bipolar episode and accidentally burnt her youngest child to death, by dropping her into a scolding oven! The media then virtually dragged my grandma to her death, as articles naming my grandma: "Beverly Burn" kept being printed and sold in the state; grandma Beverly then hung herself...

Dr J Irwin sat shocked. 'Jesus, Joy. That's a huge amount to unpack, for any functioning individual. You haven't had it easy, not one bit... at apparently any stage of your life!' the therapist admitted.

Nervously, Joy checked the time on the hanging purple on the purple painted wall.

'I had a man come in here once. He too took a bad trip on a class-A drug. Stocky man, great hair. He admitted to me that his wife of thirteen years cheated on him, with a younger, more agile male. He also told me the drug he took was brand newly imported from Chile. To cut a long story short, the man was found dead, looking like a pale vampire on the outskirts of Los Angeles. He slit his wrists, which drained all the blood out of him; as he wasn't discovered for three days. The oddest part though came from when a detective noticed his hair was cut. The man cut his hair off as a "last gift" for his child before he killed himself. He had evidently lost his mind when he found out about his wife adultering. I tell you this, so that you can realise how close you are to reality, even if you feel a billion miles away! I'm here to help you!' Dr Irwin spoke.

Each mere letter sunk into Joy's mind; for a slight moment she felt as if she could see! As if she was back in the room, with reality among her!

Dr Irwin's purple alarm dinged! Joy's session was complete.

'That's us for today, Ms Monroe. Would you like to make an appointment for another session?' said Irwin.

'I would... how much and for when, Dr Irwin?' Joy replied.

'How about next Thursday; plus, don't worry about the payment this week,' Irwin kindly replied.

Joy then left the doc's purple office, feeling much better and connected.

The person sitting where Joy sat half an hour previously had a fresh scar on his head, it looked like he was also waiting for a session with Dr Irwin.

The wheels off Joy's car burned thin as she speeded on the Reno highway, blasting Fleetwood Mac; feeling much more content.

Joe, Margaret, no one was on her mind. She focused on positivity and positivity only.

Making a pit stop, Joy parked up near a tacky brown store which sold loads of useless tat.

Joy went into the store because they sold a hidden gem: the best palo santo in Reno!

Palo santo is incense which is predominantly burned/used by the Latin-American community. It is supposedly brilliant for stopping stress and negative energy. The smell is also magnificent.

There were four little boxes of "Original Palo Santo" left in stock; she paid £3.40 for a single box; bargain if you ask me.

The holder for her palo santo incense was a marble frog. It was quite cute. The marble frog sat on a marble lillipad as it held the incense stick.

As Joy arrived home, her dad immediately questioned her in her session with her therapist, as he still felt heavily guilty for her newfound disorder; 'How'd it go?' Michael asked his daughter, as she got out of her automobile.

'Honestly... really fuckin' good!' Joy positively replied.

Michael looked like he was going to climax with how relieved he was that his little girl's therapy session went well!

Her father did a little dance; as he thought to himself that there is salvation with Joy starting therapy.

Michael hurried his daughter into her home, as he had cooked a special meal for her, a bravery food award per say: chicken parmesan.

Her vision was still blurry, and her feelings felt distant, but Joy felt like fighting, she felt like gaining back her reality with every atom within her!

The chicken parm was Michael's specialty. It was crunchy, had a hint of sweetness and was packed with sea salt! His ex-wife, Margaret of course, had very hateful criticisms toward her former husband's special dish...

'The dog's meal is tastier than this, I bet!'

'Why's my chicken soft on the inside?'

'This is horrid, Michael!' were some of Margaret's negative remarks.

It was actually a holy miracle that Michael Monroe didn't end up stabbing his ex-wife!

The chicken parm was just how Joy remembered it when she was a girl; she ate every bite, and the past two months Joy barely ate carbohydrates, meat, etcetera!

Michael gazed into his daughter's lustful, yet drained eyes and spoke to her. 'I'm proud of you.'

'Thanks, Dad,' Joy said back to her dad.

They both cleared the dishes, then Joy headed to bed for some rest.

A clear night's rest was stunning for Joy, as since she developed the disorder her sleep was horrendous, but for once Joy's sleep was bearable once more!

Morn came once again...

Joy's eyelids opened. That dreaded disassociated feeling returned! Joy was heartbroken! She felt even more disconnected. It was so very confusing.

She went from feeling as if she was beginning to improve, to waking up even worse than before. It began to break Joy, as she got out of her bed, with little motivation, as the derealisation kicked in once more!

Her reflection in her mirror looked dead, detached and desolate...

Michael was still on a high from the night before, that he was just as shocked and hurt as Joy when he found out she was feeling even worse than before, after her evidently getting better.

Her father walked into her bedroom, seeing a drained looking Joy, (he was so incredibly shocked, as it was just a mere eight hours ago his daughter was beginning to look natural again). He snapped between ecstatic to manic!

'I'm guessing you don't want... sweet potato brownies?' A shattered Michael Monroe asked Joy Monroe. His little girl looked up with a fresh, wet face and began balling her eyes out.

Michael hadn't run toward his daughter as quickly in all of his life. He grabbed her tight; 'I tried, Dad. I tried so fucking hard!' Joy yelled from deep within her fleshy lungs, 'I know, Joy,' Michael replied as he too balled his eyes out with tears as he witnessed his one and only child get her absolute soul destroyed by something he blamed on himself and couldn't find a way to fix...

And in that instant a faint noise was heard. The house's phone began silently humming as someone was trying to call the pair of them.

Joy didn't hear the phone ringing as she uncontrollably kept sobbing; Michael on the other hand did hear it.

As the ringing got louder; and Michael tried to ignore it, Joy did finally hear it.

At this stage her sadness and emptiness turned into raw anger, so she got up off her bathroom floor and charged into her living room, where her house phone dwelled.

Joy answered the phone... it was none other than her mother!

'Joy? Are you there? Honey, I'm so sore...' Her mom pleaded down the muffled telephone line before Joy aggressively smashed the telephone off the ground, destroying it and breaking it into a hundred little pieces!

Michael knew immediately who was on the other end of the phone by how shocked Joy was.

Joy got more angered by the minute; she kept stomping on the phone's broken pieces as she roared like a rancid bear.

Her dad had to intervene; he couldn't stand seeing his daughter like that.

'Why won't it go away!' Joy roared. It was the loudest Michael ever heard his daughter; the walls around them had a slight rumble with the scale of her roar.

Half an hour later, Joy began becoming emotionally exhausted. She had no more tears left to yearn.

Sporadically her dad picked her up and took her to her car. The night's sky was black as coffee.

The dusty sound of her car's engine turning on gave Joy the energy to utter a word. 'I'm sorry, Dad,' hopelessly Joy admitted.

As soon as Michael heard his daughter state something like that, he drove straight out of the driveway and had the deepest, most loving discussion with his little girl.

The sad, yet miserable truth was that Joy acted like she took every ounce of what her dad had to say, but in reality her disorder made her disconnect from virtually everything at that point. She was at all-time low. Her father cried, laughed, sang... he did whatever it took to try and help and break his daughter from her dissociative state; her mind deceived her to think that there was no salvation. Joy Monroe was broken...

Joy acted as if she was happier; as if what her father said truly, internally touched and healed her.

Their drive lasted until deep into the morning; the time Michael drove home was 04:20pm.

As the pair entered the house, they both were physically and mentally exhausted. Michael stared into his daughter luscious eyes once more; and said to Joy, 'You know you're a bright, beautiful, talented, glamorous girl. Your eccentric therapist has all the hope in the world for you. You could have any man in Reno. You truly are a fucking inspiration. I love you... I'm so proud of you!' – Joy then teared, hugged her father as tight as humanly possible, kissed his forehead and wished him goodnight.

Joy entered her bedroom. Her blinds were open so the blinding city lights of Reno were visible to see.

She looked into her mirror and saw once again a blurred reflection.

Joy had a small makeup stool in her room.

She pulled it out into the centre of her bedroom, where a fan laid upon her bedroom ceiling.

Joy then removed her beloved Vivienne Westwood necklace from around her chest and wrapped it around her fan as she also wrapped it around her neck.

Joy stepped onto the small makeup stool.

She breathed in three vast breaths.

She kicked the stool with one of her feet.

Quickly she began choking.

Her neck was bruised badly.

Blood flowed from her eyes, mouth and nose.

Everything was turning black.

Almost all of her oxygen left her.

Her feet rapidly moved forwards and backwards… until they stopped.

Joy Monroe had hung herself.

The aftermath was disturbing.

Joy's bruised, bloodied dead corpse swayed slowly from left to right.

Her favourite necklace which she used to kill herself was almost broken as her weight was wearing it.

Reno's city lights kept blinking, as if nothing had happened.

A thud was made. The Vivienne Westwood necklace couldn't hold Joy's dead body any longer. Her corpse whacked the wooden floor hard.

A single pearl from the necklace bounced off of Joy's bloodied face and rolled onto a desk which had a framed photo of a smiling, happy version of herself.

The pearl was dyed with Joy's blood; it rolled over to the picture of her.

A brief twinkle emerged from the single bloodied Vivienne Westwood pearl. The twinkle then got covered by falling rubble.

The weight of Joy broke her weak ceiling.
The ceiling tumbled down onto her corpse.

THE END

Printed in Great Britain
by Amazon